CW00842523

2007
Mini Saga Competition
Young Writers
in association with
STAEDTLER

mini
S·A·G·A·S·

Hampshire Tales

First published in Great Britain in 2007 by
Young Writers, Remus House, Coltsfoot Drive,
Peterborough, PE2 9JX
Tel (01733) 890066 Fax (01733) 313524
All Rights Reserved

© Copyright Contributors 2007
SB ISBN 978-1-84431-324-2

Foreword

Young Writers was established in 1991, with the aim of encouraging the children and young adults of today to think and write creatively. Our latest secondary school competition, 'Mini S.A.G.A.S.', posed an exciting challenge for these young authors: to write, in no more than fifty words, a story encompassing a beginning, a middle and an end. We call this the mini saga.

Mini S.A.G.A.S. Hampshire Tales is our latest offering from the wealth of young talent that has mastered this incredibly challenging form. With such an abundance of imagination, humour and ability evident in such a wide variety of stories, these young writers cannot fail to enthral and excite with every tale.

Contents

The Mini Sagas

The Visit

He arrives, we go into the kitchen. 'Well I'd better get started,' bringing out the tube of lubricating gel and smearing it over everything, thrusting and groaning. Then he finishes. '£100 please love.'
'£100 for that?'
'Well, there's the cost of the parts and a call out charge.'
Bloody plumbers!

Emily Constable (18)
Barton Peveril College

13

The Scary Story

When it was pitch-black the fear was shivering down my spine. The cold graveyard had lots of spooky noises. I felt a cold air draught on my shoulder. The noises got louder, the flinching of my body got worse and worse. I scooped towards the gate, I screamed

...

Amber Geach (12)
Brune Park Community College

A Man

I met a man. We talked, he joked, I laughed, we parted at my stop. I phoned for a taxi. I looked behind, he was there, I ran, I ran, I hid. He was there. I ran, I ran, a cliff, I fell.
He looked over the edge, he laughed.

Lauran McCalmont (12)
Brune Park Community College

15

The Unlucky Lake

When I was sitting by a lake a baby crocodile jumped from the lake. I climbed the nearest tree. Suddenly I realised that I disturbed a beehive. I smacked the crocodile with my shoe. He screamed and hit the tree. The beehive fell on my head and I dropped unconscious.

Richard Prihradsky (12)
Brune Park Community College

16

World War IV

I sat there alone in the trench, bombs going off around me. Death must have been busy today. Why did I trust the stupid army? Suddenly, the sky was filled with a spaceship dropping, yet more alien troops. One of them landed in front of me. My war was over.

Connor Cadogan (13)
Brune Park Community College

The Door Handle

Amber took hold of the door handle. Her heart started to skip a few beats. Sweat poured off her head as she turned the handle in a clockwise direction. It seemed like the door hadn't been opened in at least a few years. Her head spinning, her heart thumping.

'Help!'

Rachel Honey (13)
Brune Park Community College

18

What?

I reached for the door handle, it opened with a creak. There was a cackle of laughter. My heart stopped as I reached to open the lounge door. I got my head around the door and saw my daughter looking horrified. I jumped to see Miss Hooly from Balamory! Cringe!

Victoria Smith (13)
Brune Park Community College

The Nightmare

Brogan stared at the door. Her palms started to sweat, her breath came in short shallow bursts. The handle turned slowly. Brogan stepped back. The opening was like a slow death. There he stood, the man from Brogan's nightmares. Only he wasn't a nightmare anymore! A scream echoed around.

Lucy Wood (13)
Brune Park Community College

Death

I walk upstairs. My parents' room door looks hot. I walk up to it. I can hear heavy breathing like a fire. The light behind the door looks like fire. My first intention is to run, run, run. But I can't move. I turn the doorknob. It opens. Hell awaits …

Elliot Dudgeon (13)
Brune Park Community College

The Murder Of Emily Rose

Emily was your average girl, she was always helpful
to everyone, but something happened that would
change everyone's lives. While on her way home, she
realised she was being followed. She tried to run but
she tripped over. Before she could get up someone
was over her. He murdered her.

Charlotte Weffman (12)
Brune Park Community College

Child's Play

Revenge is contagious, so is hate. That's how the war of VPR started. No one died but at the end of the day we won. All the injuries suffered were grazed knees and damage to the enemy's monster ego. Our mums complained but we didn't care, we won.

Chenin Parsons (12)
Brune Park Community College

23

Orphan Basketball Player

There was a smallish boy and he was an orphan and his name was Mike. He always dreamt of being in the MBA. He had a friend, he trained him very well. Mike wasn't good at first, but when his friend came he was very good. He wore magic shoes.

Zoe Jessey (12)
Brune Park Community College

24

Haunted House

It was very dark. I was running in the forest near the old house. I didn't run into it. I thought, *I'm running in the other direction*, but I wasn't. I was getting closer. I bashed into its door, I ran inside and saw him laying dead on the floor.

Daria Ochwat (12)
Brune Park Community College

The Nightmare Dentist

We're here in the waiting room. 'Come in.'
'Gulp!'
'Right, take a seat.'
A shiver up my spine. All thoughts in my head gone.
He turned on the drill.
'It won't hurt a bit.'
'Argh!'
I got up, I felt sick. My puffy fat cheek told the story.

Bradley Archer (12)
Brune Park Community College

B'day

'Happy b'day.'
I glanced around. Pink, purple etc balloons
everywhere. I unwrapped the first prezzie I saw.
'Wow, Playboy pens.'
Later at school. 'Wow, I love them,' Amanda said.
She was so jealous. After break they were gone -
lost. My mum and dad would be mad at me.

Charlotte Higgon (12)
Brune Park Community College

Scare In The Museum

There's a museum in London. A girl had a job to look after it. At night a group of girls put sensors on the artefacts and caused them to be alive. She found it was her enemies. She also played the same trick on them and they went out screaming.

Jessica Daw (12)
Brune Park Community College

28

Bang In The Night

Bang! I woke up clutching my sheets, then again *bang!*
I slowly got out of bed, I walked down the stairs.
Creak! I thought nothing of it.
'What was that?'
I felt a cold chill. I started to run, then suddenly. *'Argh, Mum!'*
In the morning I was found dead!

Eleanor Tobin (12)
Brune Park Community College

29

Night At The Cinema

As I walked into the cinema people gave me filthy, cruel and mean looks. I went and sat down and I felt something prickly down my back. I turned around. *Bam*, one went flying in my face. I followed them out to the toilets then I chucked popcorn at them.

Paris Evans (12)
Brune Park Community College

30

Untitled

A man, quite young, he looked at me. He smiled and didn't look at all worried. I looked down - the ski slope was huge. I was pushed. A tree and another, mist. The end of the cliff, 'Oh no, stop!' I fell. 'Game over,' said my game console.

Chloe Smith (11)
Brune Park Community College

Untitled

We all gathered into the helicopter, guns set and ready for action. We were up and running and flying over their bases. Our infantry devastated, people lying in pools of blood. Infantry taking valuable shelter. Some people were lucky, survivors. All of us left giving medical attention to the team.

Cameron Giffon (12)
Brune Park Community College

32

Graveyard Mum

That night in the graveyard I went to the place my mum said to meet. There was a light, it was her. She looked weird. Dripping like she'd been swimming, her hair long and black was over her face. She touched me, I froze to my death, never to wake.

Emma Ward (12)
Brune Park Community College

Walking Through The Graveyard

Walking through the graveyard I saw light, it didn't
look normal light, it was bright and shiny. It came
closer, there was a lady, transparent. In shock I said,
'I only came out for a walk, I don't mean any harm.'
Stumbling back my heart beat faster, I was scared.

Molly Dore (12)
Brune Park Community College

34

That Night

The night; pitch-black. I was not alone, it was freezing cold. Then suddenly I heard a voice. The voice murmured, calling out to me, I was trembling and tears were coming down my cheeks. I could not bear it anymore.

Boo! It pounced out. I stood paralysed. I knew.

Oakley Evans (12)
Brune Park Community College

The Long Night

The darkness was almost ghostly, some nights I wished for the day to come sooner. Looking out, sparkling water under the moon. Imagining mermaids jumping out at any time, but the waves came in and the waves washed out. The mermaids didn't come that night, but something else came instead.

Lucy Webb (12)
Brune Park Community College

A Nervous Day

The day was Monday, the first day of the week, the worst day. My knees were clattering together, I'm in school, where is he? My head turned left and right. No sight of him. School flew by, the end of the day and school was over. No bully. I'm safe.

Thomas Whaley (12)
Brune Park Community College

37

Impossible

As the team lowered side to side, avoiding the tripwires I was first down. I carefully ran to the case and lifted the glass. I transferred the diamond into the bag, then ran to the wire, zipped up and I was away with the diamond.

Joshua Wright (12)
Brune Park Community College

Down The Alley

I was jogging down the alley, it was pitch-black. I was a little scared but not much. I caught some rustling, I glimpsed something but didn't know what it was. I wanted to see what it was. Then it rustled again, it jumped out and grabbed me.

'Argh! Help!'

Kayleigh Porter (12)
Brune Park Community College

The Last Kick

It's a sunny Saturday and I'm at the Sunderland vs Newcastle game. After 80 minutes the score is 1-1 and it's starting to get intense. Here comes extra time and Sunderland win a penalty - the new striker Sunderland bought for £20,000,000 shoots and scores. They're through to the Champions League.

Conor Ryan (12)
Brune Park Community College

40

Drama In English

Last Tuesday a fifty ton weight fell through the English classroom ceiling squashing a pupil. The girl's recovering well in hospital and hasn't been named. (She is slightly shorter than before!) Hospital staff have informed her she'll soon be released but may have to do therapy to remove initial shock.

Emily Baldwin (13)
Farnborough Hill School

A Field Trip

'Jessica, Jess! Over here. Hurry, otherwise you're going to miss the smelly coach ride on this rotten bus.' It was a cold, frosty, February morning and Woking High School were on an extremely boring field trip to the Natural History Museum. It was going to be a very interesting occasion …

Georgia Peel (13)
Farnborough Hill School

42

Jason

Cara stared blankly at the blank page: Jason's face swam into her mind. His tanned arms wrapped protectively around her. His blue eyes were just a few inches above hers. She imagined seeing them look away, willingly to a pretty young model who was walking away from them. He followed.

Frances Plowman (15)
Farnborough Hill School

Silent Tongues

She stood oblivious of her surroundings, in a world
of her own: no sounds, smells, just the sense of sight.
However, she could tell their bitter tongues from
their gestures and spiteful-looking faces. Her head
was spinning. The bullying got too much. She was
gasping and finally fainted. Silence!

Lauren Edmondson (13)
Farnborough Hill School

44

Shiver And Shake Me Awake

It started again, but never went away! I think it's here to stay. It rumbles and crumbles, chattering away all night long. It just sits there, never moving, never seeing and never thinking. It scares me. I shake and shiver.

This is the sound of Grandpa Jim smoking his pipe!

Claire Gujer (13)
Farnborough Hill School

45

Picked My Weeds And Kept The Flowers

Beyond it all she knew she needed to let go. She had to leave the past behind. She stepped out of the darkness and through the fire and touched the flame. She had held on for too long, but she knew she could never forget and fully leave it all.

Anakalia Phillips (13)
Farnborough Hill School

Cheerleading Chills

On came the cheerleaders in full spirit, ready to begin. The crowd went wild. 'Ready? OK!' yelled Tarla, the Bulldog's captain. 'Bulldogs' fans in the stands, are you ready to *yell* and cheer?' One stunt group loaded up, ready to explode. 'Go Red!' As they threw, the girl fell, *dead!*

Alice Crutchfield (13)
Farnborough Hill School

The Tale Of The Black Cat

The sleek black cat carefully jumped up onto a stack of books on the old oak bookshelf. As the books toppled the cat did another daring jump onto the window sill. The cat tried to grip the window, but soon realised it was open and fell out onto the trampoline.

Nikki Golder (13)
Farnborough Hill School

Help!

'You can't do this to me!' she screamed and he slammed the door. She heard him lock it, and then there was nothing, just emptiness. The ropes wrapped around her were getting tighter and tighter. She closed her eyes and the room was filled with the sounds of the night.

Sophie Came (13)
Farnborough Hill School

49

The Jump

Phil Ince grasped hold of the mountain and grimaced. He stared down at the ground and felt sick; how high was he? Suddenly he slipped, losing his grip. Phil sighed and quickly grabbed hold of the edge, pulling himself to the top. He took a deep breath and jumped. Freedom!

Gabrielle King (13)
Farnborough Hill School

The Fiery Red-Head

Kate stared at the blank page: Jason's face swam into her mind. His tanned arms wrapped around her. His blue eyes gazed across the page and looked up. There she was, just walking down the corridor. He ran after her leaving Kate. He was attracted to her fiery red hair.

Jess Deans (15)

Farnborough Hill School

Today's The Day!

Serenity looked up from her English paper. Fifteen minutes left and only the comprehension finished! *I'm going to fail,* she thought disappointedly. Her sister had told her that today she would pass, but Serenity knew it wouldn't happen. *Today would be special,* Serenity thought. It was, but for something different

. . .

Francesca Pipkin (12)
Farnborough Hill School

Man Overboard!

The ship jerked from side to side in the rolling waves.
The sailors were tossed here and there. The captain
sat snug in his cabin: nice and dry, watching the
sailors struggling to climb the rigging and tie down
the cargo. One sailor tripped, falling into the raging
waves, *splash!*

Lucy Chisnaff (12)
Farnborough Hill School

53

One Step

I stepped one pace at a time, not knowing why I was trying to be quiet. One more pace and again. A whispering voice was muttering behind me. 'Izzy.' I suddenly stopped, peered behind me and was very scared at this point in time. I looked once more and screamed.

Emily-Isabelle Morris (13)
Farnborough Hill School

Just Three Words

The sun slowly sank down into the calm blue sea and I turned to look at the boy next to me. His piercing green eyes stared straight into mine and I knew he wanted to say exactly the same as me. The three most meaningful words that can be said …

Georgie Tate (12)
Farnborough Hill School

Tragedy!

One day I was walking along the beach when in the distance I realised something coming fairly fast and furious, aiming at me! I started to stumble towards the edge of the pavement platform; suddenly I fell off and landed flat on my face! *Ouch!* All for a charging animal.

Laura Haines (13)
Farnborough Hill School

Things Are Not As They Seem

She stood in the darkness underneath street light.
Where was he? she thought to herself. She waited
another ten minutes before giving up all hope and
trudging home. She turned the corner and gasped in
horror; there he was holding a gun.
'Going somewhere?' he said in a harsh voice.

Joanna Fuller (13)
Farnborough Hill School

57

A Man And A Wristwatch

Albert had a wristwatch. His life was run by it; his life changed when it stopped. When he reset it two minutes fast, he arrived at the bus stop early. A boy riding a bike skidded in front of the bus: Albert rushed in the way and he died instead.

Freya-Anne Robertson (13)
Farnborough Hill School

58

The Ugly Princess

Among beautiful palaces and mountains far, far away, there lived a princess. She wasn't an ordinary princess though, not the type who wore dresses and ball gowns. She was ugly, obese, green and ate like a monster. However, she had a good heart, although everyone judged her by her looks.

Becky Wilson (13)
Farnborough Hill School

Ghost Of A Girl

It's strange I'm always ignored. It's weird how I feel.
A car nearly hit me but it didn't hurt. Last time it
hurt. In the kitchen, Mum's crying. She doesn't notice
me. 'She's gone,' she sobs. 'She's gone!'
'I'm here,' I reply. She hears nothing. Why does that
keep happening?

Charlotte Waldron (13)
Farnborough Hill School

Bullied Or Suspended

I walked into the school courtyard. There they were.
Immediately laughing, jeering … bullying! Hold your
head high!
'Where'd you think you're going?'
I remembered that pain, hurt, rejection … not again,
not ever. One mistake, brought me this, this life, this
horror, this bullying … Do I take it or leave it?

Emma Hopkins (13)

Farnborough Hill School

A Surge Of Power

Alone in a field. A dark sky descending. A crash, a flash of light. A surge of power. I fell, limp, helpless, paralysed. I looked left there stood a man. Why didn't he help me? A policeman? They had caught me, I had been shot with a laser gun.

Victoria Watt (13)
Farnborough Hill School

The Noise Downstairs

There was a crash downstairs. We heard tumbling about. My friends and I slowly crept out of bed, onto the landing. We realised one of my friends had gone, what if the thing downstairs had got her? I raced down to find her … 'Oh, I was just getting a drink!'

Gabriella Ezzard (13)
Farnborough Hill School

Dream Coma

MY eyes were closed, I could hear a beeping machine. I opened my eyes, doctors' faces examining me. 'You have been in a coma for twenty years, you are thirty-two years old Laura.'
'What? Mum is it true?'
'It's time to get up now.'
Phew, what a strange dream.

Lily Bennett (13)
Farnborough Hill School

64

The Mysteries Of The Wood

Deep, dark night. A rustling, a silence, a man tiptoed across rustling leaves. He felt something brush past. He spun around, nothing. Again a rustling, a flash of white, what is it? Music, deep, rhythmical, getting louder, faster. The world spinning. Blackout, wake up, sore head. Light, bright, good.

Natalie Sears (13)
Farnborough Hill School

65

Bang!

As I walked down that long alley, I could hear the sound of footsteps. Then I heard the sound of a trigger from behind. 'Put your hands up where I can see them. Empty your pockets!' I put my hand in my pocket and *bang!* I shot him. Oh dear.

Jade Davies (13)
Farnborough Hill School

Cheat

'Janice Dickens, what are you staring at?' Clues were there, mouth open, eyes staring at it. 'How dare you, I won't have it, I never thought you could think of such a thing.'

My cheeks blushed red with shame. There it was, my GCSE paper, torn to shreds. 'You cheater!'

Mahim Husnain (13)
Farnborough Hill School

Walking On A Volcano

It was a barren place, crunching underfoot. Hot and cold, it's bright up here, so high like being a god, looking down on one's kingdom. It smelt of things from deep within the Earth. Perhaps a whiff of Hell. Mock if you like, but not up here. Etna is queen.

Sarah Wilson (13)
Farnborough Hill School

A Chilling Tale!

After the party, Lizzy grabbed her keys to drive but felt a sudden feeling of impending doom! Something said, *'Don't drive!'* She took a taxi instead. Once home she had a call from an anxious friend. 'You OK? I've had a nightmare! You had a car accident.' Lizzy felt chilled!

Rebecca Henderson (13)
Farnborough Hill School

The Girl Next Door

The removal van arrived and then was gone, my best friend along with it. Sadly I looked out of my window and watched as a new van pulled into next door. A girl emerged. She saw me and smiled. Maybe it wasn't going to be a bad summer after all …

Rianna Mezzuffo (13)
Farnborough Hill School

The Noise On The Landing

I couldn't sleep. I was scared. I hid under my duvet.
Creaking floorboards came from the landing. Was
someone out there? I crept out of bed and opened
my door. Two glowing green eyes stared at me from
the shadows, moving slowly towards me, ready to
grab me and … 'Miaow.'

Philippa Lewis (13)
Farnborough Hill School

My End

I could feel my life slowly slipping away. I was done for. 'Why don't you just kill me?' I shouted to the person next to me.

'Kill you, why would I do that?' they smiled enigmatically. This is it. Time to face my end. The Monday morning school bell rang.

Eleanor Davey-Rogerson (13)
Farnborough Hill School

How We Met

'How do you get to Albert Street?' he asked as he grabbed my arm with his silk-like hands.
'Down the road, turn right,' I said glaring into his luscious brown eyes.
'Thanks love, you going my way?'
'Can do.'
Got his name and number. He's now my gorgeous husband!

Lara Badgery (13)
Farnborough Hill School

73

My Life Is Hell

Me and my siblings have been in foster homes mostly.
We're back with Mum now in a bed and breakfast.
The people are horrible, especially Kelly, she bullies
me. She calls me names, looks down her nose at me.
No problem though, after all, we won the lottery
that evening.

Hannah Watkins (13)
Farnborough Hill School

74

A Usual Day

Usual day. Same people, same surroundings, different feelings. My body felt out of place like heavy clouds on my shoulders. Carried on my day normally and went home as normal. No awareness what my future was going to hold. In the morning I lived. In a year I was dead.

Charlotte Arnold (13)

Farnborough Hill School

One Night

Last night ... a horrific thing happened. It was a dark gloomy night, the wind was howling. A calm man came into the fish and chip shop, the window was broken, furniture was ripped, but worst of all the fish got battered!

Jai Jackman (11.3)
Farnborough Hill School

Under The Sea

Two best friends. One had rich blonde hair and sea-blue eyes. The other had mud-coloured hair and dark chocolate eyes. Swimming in the sea when one of them felt a tug on her leg. A blink of an eye and she was gone. Eaten by a shark.

Chloe Gallagher (13)
Farnborough Hill School

Lost And Found

I didn't usually leave things about. These were also
my favourite sunglasses. I scanned the classroom but
only saw books. *Mum won't be happy*. I thought as
I entered the canteen. She'd bought them for me.
Suddenly I saw Jenny coming towards me.
'Hey Emma, I've found these new sunglasses!'

Olivia Stilwell (13)
Farnborough Hill School

Naïve

'Where you goin'?' An attractive man pulled up in a Mercedes.

'Glassi Bar,' I responded flirtatiously.

'Jump in,' he said simply flashing a smile.

Surprised by his refreshing confidence I did trustingly.

He put his foot on it and locked the doors.

'Buckle up, you're in for a bumpy ride …'

Dannielle Dhaliwal (13)

Farnborough Hill School

Betrayal Of The Heart

Cara stared blankly at the blank page: Jason's face swam into her mind. His tanned arms wrapped protectively around her. His blue eyes twinkled in the light. Then out of the window Cara saw Jason, stood up in gladness. However, Jess appeared alongside Jason, they kissed. Cara's heart shattered.

Janet Chambers (14)
Farnborough Hill School

The Man At The Door

Jess stumbled down the stairs. The figure at the
door continued knocking. 'I'm coming,' she shouted.
She turned on the porch light and opened the door.
Standing there was a tall dark figure, her father.
'What are you doing here?'
'I'm here to be your father.'
She closed the door.

Cara Stevenson (14)
Farnborough Hill School

81

It

He ran for miles and miles. The woods were cold.
It was ahead of him, a tall black figure towered over
him. He was soon lying on the floor, warm blood
clung to his head. As the thing moved towards him
he caught a glimpse of sharp teeth. Then nothing.

Oliver Hughes (13)
Horndean Technology College

What Was That?

I was lying in bed. It was one minute to one. The wind was howling, I heard a sudden bang, clatter, thud. Then silence. I crept out of bed. Beads of nervous sweat saturating my clothes. I approached the kitchen. To my relief it was my mum, she was thirsty.

Robyn Tiffer (15)
Horndean Technology College

Black Beauty

A sunny morning in a place called Horndead. Some sort of animal was reborn. It was black all over with a little star. The years went by, it got older and turned into a black stallion that would stand on his back legs and rear up as he was released.

Hannah Searle (12)
Horndean Technology College

All The Fun In The World

Spinning, screaming, smoke! Followed by an almighty roar! Now getting pushed harder into your seat, you have to ease. Now being swung about with a slide, with aggression in your head and roar outside. You are now even more determined to finish a lap of go-karting!

Matt Tilbury (13)
Horndean Technology College

The Boy's Friend

'Hi,' said Harry to his friend. 'How are you?'
'I'm fine thanks,' said the boy's friend. Another
boy walked over cautiously saying hello as he
approached.
'Who are you talking to?' asked the boy.
'My friend,' said Harry.
The boy stared at Harry as if he was mad. 'Where?'

Alex Murphy (13)
Horndean Technology College

86

The New Drifter

A 19 year-old raced people in America. One day he crashed while racing someone. He got charged by the police. He had to move to Tokyo. He went to live with his dad. Most people drift so he learnt how to drift and became the best drifter in Tokyo.

Siân Price (13)
Horndean Technology College

87

No Way Out

The abandoned deserted hospital came to life that night. Your worst enemy became your best. Your best became one of them. As you rush down the stairs trying to get off that floor you are still on it. You see spirits and shadows strolling around you, you're petrified.

Charlotte Fagg (13)
Horndean Technology College

88

The Emigration

All packed in, all ready. Off they went in a cloud of smoke. Left the old and entered the new. Nothing will stop them now. Soon they were tired, pulled over and rested but little did they know they were back where they started. They took a look and stayed.

Jamie Saunders (13)
Horndean Technology College

Revenge

The man was very angry because the King of England killed my wife. I started a rebellion to kill the King from Scotland to England. I took some land from him, we fought all day and night. Finally he fell to my sword and I became King of the south.

Shane Pinches (13)
Horndean Technology College

The House

The windows were boarded up and the house was dark. There was a loud bang from the attic. We made for the door but I was grabbed and thrown to the floor. I felt the quick slash of a knife striking my neck. I choked on my own blood.

Michael Miller (13)
Horndean Technology College

91

The Motorbike

'Are you okay?' James said. Ben fell off the motorbike.
'Yes, I'm fine,' laughed Ben.
'I think it went too high and chucked you off.'
frowned James.
'Yeah, I know,' said Ben.
'Stupid arcade machines that really worried me,'
James whispered.
They both laughed and went home.

Emma Fowler (12)
Horndean Technology College

92

The Deadly Knock

I heard a bang at the door. I looked through the hole. Nothing was there. Suddenly a light shone in my face. A pain in my belly as sharp as a knife. I looked down - there was blood. I fell back and I started to fade. The ghost moved away.

Jessica Green (13)
Horndean Technology College

93

The Ghost

Mark walked through the house feeling wary that he wasn't alone. He looked round, he heard a noise from the attic. He opened the door and there stood a man.
'Who are you?'
'I'm John, I'm here to haunt you!'
Mark fainted, John laughed.

Marie Jafkins (13)
Horndean Technology College

94

Stuck There

In there waiting and waiting. Some people have just come back, now it is my turn. I picked up my weapon and just wait with my friends of four. The light shines on my face as they all look at us. The gig begins and I play my part tonight.

Harry Phelan (13)
Horndean Technology College

95

Instant Action

I was strolling through the woods when a Minotaur lashed at me out of a cave. I panicked and hid behind a rock. Strangely there was a shield and sword there. I picked them up and attacked the beast. I slashed at its neck and it died a bloody death!

Ben Johnson (13)
Horndean Technology College

Dance Of The Year

The rivals stepped forward into the blinding light. I look around to find my partner. Where was he? Our music started pumping as I stepped out on the stage. My partner awaited, adrenaline rushed through my body as his gleam looked me in my eyes.

Kirsty Richmond (13)
Horndean Technology College

Jokers

Two people are sitting in an average park on a wall. One of them tells a joke, the other falls off. The joke teller does it again the next day to someone else but this boy doesn't fall. I guess he didn't get the 'punch' line!

Ruby Trimby (14)
Horndean Technology College

The Bin

The night was coming fast. The owls were calling. I smelt a bad smell like someone had not brushed their teeth. The smell was paralysing. Mum shouted at me to empty the bin for once in my life.

Sasha Sherrard (14)
Horndean Technology College

99

Footballer

He woke up one morning and decided he wanted to be a footballer. From then, he always had a football in his hands day and night. When he was in bed and even when he was at school. Then one day he got bored and never played football ever again.

George Purnell (14)
Horndean Technology College

100

The Cat That Liked Milk And Cat Food Who Fell Down A Well

There was a cat who liked milk and cat food. One day he went out to play with the other animals but fell down a big well. The farmer went to look for the cat and found him two days later and got the cat out with a long rope.

Matthew Turner (14)
Horndean Technology College

The Riddle Of The Earth

They lay on the beach, they lay by the lake. They sit on a mountain, they sink into the sea. They go to parties and sit on display. Some come with friends, some come alone. Some live deep underground, but what they all have in common - they come from Earth.

Sam Thompson (14)
Horndean Technology College

Dead End

I ran, panting as I went. I was so tired, I could have collapsed but the fear kept me going. I turned a corner and tripped on the kerb. I got up and turned another corner, but the horror had found me. I hit a dead end.

Corey Honess (14)
Horndean Technology College

Reserve

He's running and running towards the sea to reserve their lives. He hears the voice saying, 'Help.' He's swimming and drowning in the ocean but can't swim. He's drowning and drowning. Suddenly he wakes up and hears someone saying, 'Are you OK?'

Mafsin Ahmed (14)
Horndean Technology College

The Tunnel

Me and my friend walked into a tunnel. He said,
'What was that?'
'I don't know,' I said.
He turned around and there were some glowing
eyes in the shadows - *bang!* Then he was gone. I
called his name, 'Jeff, Jeff.' There was no answer. I
turned and ran.

Ben Clarke (14)
Horndean Technology College

Untitled

There were two kids in the back. They were so scared they turned the corner at 100mph. The one on the left Jim, couldn't hear his friend. He thought he would die as he heard the scream of his friend. Then the ride stopped.

Tom Scott (14)
Horndean Technology College

The Room

The room. A TV with a blue screen. All is silent. The screen goes deep blood-red and shows 'They will devour everything' in flashing light … Then sudden darkness. I hear a noise. Getting closer. Hungry. I stand, unable to move.

Matthew Ingaff (14)
Horndean Technology College

Whoopee Cushion

One sunny day there lived a boy. He said his name was Ryan. He went to sit on the chair but as he sat down he farted. Everyone laughed, ha, ha, ha. He started to laugh as well. He did not notice he had sat on a whoopee cushion.

Natalie Hayward (12)
Horndean Technology College

The Rain Man

The children were running outside. It started pouring down. Nobody went inside … until their parents called them. One boy got shut out and someone was coming. The man grabbed him and took him to his house. He turned the lights on and it was just his dad. 'Thank God!'

Wiff McKenna (12)
Horndean Technology College

Krabby Patty Formula

I wanted the krabby patty formula but I couldn't do it. They caught me, they picked me up by my feet. I was hanging, I was wriggling but I couldn't break free. Three hours later I was whooshing away up and up. Then I shuddered, I didn't know what happened.

Amy Edwards (12)
Horndean Technology College

London Bombings

There I was walking down the street when I heard
an explosion. Sirens started to go off! Next second I
knew London was in ruins. I ran and heard screams.
Something fell out of the sky … the bomb exploded,
how many days were left?

Aaron Broomfield (12)
Horndean Technology College

Bang!

I was on my way to the shops when suddenly I heard a bang! It sounded like a gun. I ducked and jumped to the floor, everyone was laughing, I wondered why. It was someone who just popped a packet of crisps! On my way out it happened again!

Peter Knight (12)
Horndean Technology College

Is There A Tomorrow?

Spine-chilling noises have haunted me with long lasting nights, not knowing if we would survive! Hearing people screaming and whimpering gave me a horrific pain in the bottom of my stomach. I thought to myself, *is there a tomorrow? Will I live to see the warm golden sun again?*

Megan Harris (12)
Horndean Technology College

Travelling To London!

I couldn't refrain fussing and worrying about the time of when I would be able to get off the train. A lady strolled over to calm me down and then suddenly started singing a lullaby to me. I was so embarrassed, but actually I fell asleep and missed my junction!

Siân Hetherington (12)
Horndean Technology College

Kill Johnny

Johnny ran, he knew that Bill would be coming soon
with his squad of deadly assassins and their Samurai
swords. He was thinking of his own bloody death.
He was so scared but he went to sleep under a tree.
He was killed in his sleep and never woke up.

Edd White (12)
Horndean Technology College

The Malteser Sea Lions And 442

The sea lions were everywhere, firing Maltesers as if they were unlimited. One of the Maltesers had penetrated 442's protection vest. He was dying. The sea lions dived upon him. I saw them rip off his limbs in an extravagant array of blood. These creatures have no weakness.

Jack Vincent-Spaff (12)
Horndean Technology College

Who's There?

One night I heard something scratching on my
window. What could it be? Could it be a vampire,
trying to suck my blood or a zombie trying to kill
me? I didn't want to find out. Then I saw a shadow
coming and then …
'Honey, can you get the cat?'

Lydia Hunt (11)
Horndean Technology College

117

The Traitor

There was a man walking his dog. He came home to find that he was burgled. He called the police. They came round. The man thought it was the man he spoke to when he was walking his dog. The police are still looking for him two weeks later.

Jack Newman (10)
Horndean Technology College

118

Dotty Cheater

Bob was a stinky old tramp who liked to play
dominoes. He challenged a rich dominoes champion
to a match with all their money betted. The tramp
won by miles but the rich man took his money back.
'Why take it back?' the tramp asked.
'We never shook on it.'

Oliver Wiffers (11)
Horndean Technology College

The Awful Trick

Argh! My boat was sinking as I went over a sharp rock and I had no help. Then suddenly in the distance I saw a helicopter to save me. They carried me up and we flew off. I was relieved though it wasn't a rescue, it was a kidnap!

Ryan Grace (11)
Horndean Technology College

Love Is In The Air

The lady went for a walk and so did the smart man.
They were daydreaming and bumped into each
other and kissed! From that they were in love and
got married and had kids and they got a big fluffy dog
called Bob and lived happily ever after!

Dan Porter (10)
Horndean Technology College

The Whistler

The man strolled down the road whistling to himself. If you looked closely you could see him fingering something in his pocket. Suddenly, a guy jumped out in front of him with a gun. Two shots and the whistler was dead. They'd done it again those cops.

Rory Falconer (10)
Horndean Technology College

The Shetland Pony

There was a Shetland pony in a field. He had no friends and was very lonely. The farmer could not play with him because he was too busy. A pony walked by and the farmer decided to buy him. He was very good. The pony had someone to play with.

Connie Ray (11)
Horndean Technology College

Murder At Home

A girl saw something sort of odd. She didn't know what it was, she was scared. She went to go and see her mum, but she was asleep. 'What shall I do?' she said with a helpless sigh. She went down into the kitchen, heard some scary voices. 'Help, *argh!'*

Abbie Heffyer (11)
Horndean Technology College

The Mysterious Man

On a darkened and mysterious night in a shadow there stood a strange figure. Suddenly a huge gunshot came from a house, then the man jumped out of the shadows and ran to the door and rammed it down and next shouted his last words, 'Freeze!'

Jack Leslie (10)
Horndean Technology College

125

The Dragon

One day on the frozen sea, there was a dragon being slayed by demons of the deep. I took my sword out and ran towards the dragon. When I got there I saw the army was after me, so I saved the dragon and ran home as fast as possible.

Dennis Brydon (11)
Horndean Technology College

The Ghostly House!

One day there was a boy called Robert, he decided to go into the old, ghostly house. Robert walked in cautiously and peered around; there was a figure who ran up the old dusty staircase. Robert shouted, 'Who's there?'
Then someone jumped out at him and he never walked again!

Robert Crabtree (11)
Horndean Technology College

Wash On-Board

One day I went with my family and boarded a ship. It was my first time on-board. I was nervous and scared. On a stormy night I heard my baby sister scream. As I came up on deck I was vigorously shaken overboard. Never seen, never heard, ever again.

Laura Tesh (11)
Horndean Technology College

There's A Car Outside

There was a car outside, a mysterious stranger was looking in the boot. He looked like Dad, but Dad was inside. I shouted, 'Intruder.' No one heard. I looked again, he was holding bags. It was Uncle Nick.

Robert Stevens (10)
Horndean Technology College

The Lord Of The Rings

As Frodo held the ring to the light a hand grabbed him from behind. It was Gollum! He screamed, 'My precious!' as Frodo fell, Sam lunged out of nowhere, throttling Gollum. Frodo threw the ring into the volcano. Gollum jumped after it and died in the fires of Mount Doom.

Thomas Haff (11)
Horndean Technology College

Deafening Screams!

Deafening screams echoed round the lonely hall, yelps, thumps, crashes and smashes created an atmosphere in the sightless room. I couldn't see anyone; just felt a ghostly presence on the hairs of my bony back.

'Found you,' shrieked a high-pitched voice.
All this over hide-and-seek!

Sam Rogers (13)
Horndean Technology College

Rain From My Eyes

Cold, empty, I had never felt these emotions so strongly before. I told Mum it was raining as she asked about my tear-streaked face, but ignored all her other 'concerned' questions. Totally heartbroken and bitter in the warm of my room, it dawned on me … I was alone.

Oktober Duffield (13)
Horndean Technology College

The Something

I stood staring into the oblivion that lay ahead of me. The nothingness that consumed everything. The only sign of something was the flickering specks of light that carpeted the space before me. It seemed they were zooming away from me, then, all of a sudden … we left the tunnel.

Jasmine Lane (13)
Horndean Technology College

Pizza Hut Pig-Out

Jim weighed thirty stone. As he waddled into Pizza Hut he noticed a new offer. 'All You Can Eat'. He paid the £12 and sat down. He enjoyed eight large pizzas, ten garlic breads and twenty-two scoops of ice cream. He was then viciously thrown out of Pizza Hut.

Ryan Way (13)
Horndean Technology College

One Stormy Night

It was sickeningly cold in the building with the wind lashing at the windows. A door slammed open apparently of its own accord. Sally let out a horrifying scream as a muscular silhouette appeared in the door frame. The director yelled, *'Cut!'* The man and woman left for lunch.

Hannah Locke (13)
Horndean Technology College

The Fin

The fin skimmed through the water, getting closer.
It was going to get me. Suddenly it started heading
in the opposite direction. Someone had dropped
some meat in the water, trying to steer its attention
away from me. The fin disappeared under the water,
towards the meat. Was I safe … ?

Sophie Laskey (13)
Horndean Technology College

Lily And Dannii

I rushed towards my best friend Lily, in the car. I didn't want her to go! The tears ran down my face, her hand up against the window as she drove away. I dropped to the floor with anger and sadness. Was I ever going to see Lily again?

Dannielle Walbridge (13)

Horndean Technology College

The Beast

As I awoke I felt the cold sharp claws press against my chest. Fear filled me like water fills a glass. I thought I was dreaming about the film I watched the night before. My eyes opened. My vision was blurred. Then Spike my bulldog Shih-tzu cross came into focus.

Mathew Griffiths (13)
Horndean Technology College

The Drop

I was battered around by the swirling winds from side to side. The rain stung our faces with every drop. One last time the wind tried to force me off. Finally, I took one last look at my mum and jumped 200ft down into the everlasting black hole.

Mike Hawley (13)
Horndean Technology College

Electrified

The lightning was getting electrified and now it was striking down. 'Oh!' I wondered as I jogged towards the sheltered area of the bus stop. The pools of water were everywhere from the previous rainfall. *Bang!* The electricity cable had crashed to the cobbled floor. Electricity turned me to dust!

Alise Pettitt (13)
Horndean Technology College

How Did He Die?

Bill was a respectful, caring and generous man. He was satisfied with himself. Right height, weight and build. This is what was mentioned at his solemn funeral by the reverential vicar. How did he die? This was the overwhelming question in everyone's minds. Murdered or suicide? How did he die?

Richard Coffier (13)
Horndean Technology College

The End Is Close

During the holidays Amy's world ended. It all started when she was shopping for her friend's birthday present. It was a normal day until she heard some commotion in Shoe Zone. So she went to investigate. It was a robbery. The burglar had a gun. *Bang!* Amy was shot - dead.

Leanne Castle (13)
Horndean Technology College

142

Ditching The Evidence ...?

Susie Blue was a quiet child. Rarely spoke; was never nasty. At least, they didn't think she was. She stood at the river and rolled a lumpy package down the bank. She then tossed in a small sharp knife. 'Poor, silly puppy. Why would he try to swallow a knife?'

Camilla Jackson (13)
Horndean Technology College

The Fright Of My Life

We got to the top, I looked down, people began to scream. The height of 4,000ft went straight through my body. The nerves began to build up. In two seconds I was going to drop. *Flash,* the photo was taken. We reached the bottom. The ride was over!

Alice Cruickshank (12)
Horndean Technology College

Ogres

'There's ogres in your house.'
Ogres, there's no such thing as ogres. He was sure of it, so we got out of bed, flew downstairs to see what it was.
'There,' he turned and pointed at the kitchen. We opened the door. It was my parents in their face masks!

Peter Southwood (14)
Horndean Technology College

145

The Beast

I walked in. He was sat there waiting. 'Still not here?' He nodded at me and started to shake. His eyes went massive. He ran and all I could hear was breathing behind me. I turned to be faced with a horrific ugly beast with blood dropping from its mouth …

Jemma Mason (14)
Horndean Technology College

A Little Girl

Someone woke me up. A girl was standing next to me, a message was left on the table. 'She's my friend's daughter, love Mum' it said. About an hour later my stomach started rumbling. My pasta was ready, I drained the pasta. She ran into me, she was badly injured.

Chloe Chan (14)
Horndean Technology College

147

Wrong Turn

Standing at the bus stop waiting to see my friends
on the next bus. It pulls up, I panic, I have no money
ready. I shuffle through my pockets, the last person
gets on. I run to get on. I pay, turn to sit down, but
where are my friends?

Harriet Ceefey (14)
Horndean Technology College

148

Untitled

It was a cold winter's evening. I started cooking tea.
Went upstairs, sat on the sofa, shivered, stopped.
Something felt strange. It started to get warmer.
Opened a window, a weird smell, burning. I climbed
out a window, I rang the fire station - smoke from
next-door's garden. A barbecue.

Leila-Rose Lynch (14)
Horndean Technology College

Werewolf

My body shook frantically, hands and feet thick with hairs, with nails shooting from each toe and finger. Sweat was pouring off my unclothed body and pains streamed down my spine. I wasn't myself anymore. I leant over and in the reflection of the river stood a werewolf!

Hannah Henderson (14)
Horndean Technology College

The Embarrassing Moment

'Excuse me,' I say as I walk out of the bathroom.
I wonder why everyone is laughing as one of them
shouts out, 'Oy, oy!'
As I turn around I realise they are laughing at me
because I have got my dress stuck in my knickers. Oh
what an embarrassment!

Jasmine Baker (13)
Horndean Technology College

Assembly

We walked into assembly like normal. Sat in my seat.
Miss Goode then came to the front. She held four
certificates in her hand. She said they were for girls'
football. My name was called. I stood up. Strolled
down. Oh no, my fly's open!

Chloe Cameron (14)
Horndean Technology College

152

True Love!

She was fat. He was skinny. She was ugly, he was handsome. She was in love, he didn't know her name. She approached him, she stuttered, he laughed. She ran, she tripped. He laughed. She cried herself to sleep hearing his laugh. True love?

Ofivia May (13)
Horndean Technology College

The Unknown Girl

Long blonde hair. Tall slim figure. Dresses like she's something no one else is. Her voice … calm but desperate. Her movements, subtle and slow, she's everywhere I am, she takes no notice. No one knows … who is she? … The face does not exist, does this girl exist?

Coral Horn (14)
Horndean Technology College

154

Silent Murder

The door slammed as the man stumbled over. There was a loud noise coming from upstairs. As he went to check it out, a gush of wind hit him. As he went upstairs, he saw blood, he went into a room to see his wife dead on the ground!

Jordan Richards (14)
Horndean Technology College

Head Teacher

He was in my way. I shoved him, I swore at him.
'Who do you think you are talking to me like that?'
I kicked him. 'Who do you think you are? Move!'
I turned around, it was my head teacher. He said,
'Detention!'

Jamie-Lee Martin (13)
Horndean Technology College

The Train

The clouds were black. The thunder was loud. The lightning was bright as we neared the end of the track, the train stopped. The lights turned out. I heard a bang from the back of the train and everyone came rushing forward. What had happened? I didn't understand.

Laura Burreff (13)
Horndean Technology College

157

Mortar

Boom, mortars exploded around me. I ran dodging and ducking. Trees splintered, men were sent flying into the air. Ahead of me a foxhole in which four men were cowering. I jumped for it narrowly missing being hit by a mortar. Later five bodies were found scorched in a foxhole.

Scott Randall (13)
Horndean Technology College

Untitled

I was running through the woods. It was still chasing me. I shouted, it carried on. I kept running - it got closer and closer. I tripped, I turned round. A dark figure stood there, it licked my face, a dog?

Liam Dyer (13)
Horndean Technology College

The Dream

I was sleeping, dreaming about my life in the future.
Being rich; being famous. Owning everything in the
world. I was the best; the greatest. I had everything.
Suddenly, I started falling on and on in a dark and
black endless hole. I woke up!

David Hiffman (13)
Horndean Technology College

The Sneaky Spider

The sneaky spider crawled down its amazing web.
A fly got caught in the sneaky spider's amazing web.
The sneaky spider sneakily crawled along his web,
nearer and nearer to the fly. The sneaky spider
lunged at the fly. The sneaky spider was grasping the
fly. The fly got away.

Casey Brown (13)
Horndean Technology College

The Mysterious Oak

There was a sharp wind that night on the top of the creepy old oak hill. Fred had to cycle along the hill from school back to home. As he went past the old oak there was an odd rumble. Suddenly, the ground cracked. He was never seen alive again.

Josh Raper (13)
Horndean Technology College

Room On The Fifth Floor

Nobody goes to the room on the fifth floor. The last person that went was found lying dead on the bed. Three doors down only screaming was heard. Two days later someone was found dead. The people that were supposed to be dead were alive and standing next to me.

Emma Giles (13)
Horndean Technology College

Untitled

I killed a thousand people. I watched them fall to the
ground in agony as each bullet tore through their
skulls. I stuck a bomb in a Mafia hideout. *Boom,* it was
gone.
'Jack, stop playing your video games and come to
supper.'
'OK Mum, I'm coming.'

David Walker (13)
Horndean Technology College

164

The School Play

I was on the stage doing a performance 'Cinderella'. Everyone stared at me, everyone looked. I did try to say my line. I knew the words for it but they wouldn't come out of my mouth. I could feel myself falling backwards, then crash! I was looking at the floor!

Charlotte Bucknole (13)
Horndean Technology College

The Laughing Girl

One day, there was a little girl. She was laughing in hysterics on the floor. I asked, 'What are you laughing at?'
'Someone just told me the funniest joke I've ever heard, do you want me to tell you it?'
When she told me, I was on the floor laughing.

Sophie Baker (13)
Horndean Technology College

166

What's Happened?

I met a guy that night. At the town, near the stream. He seemed really nice so I invited him round. It was good until midnight came, I woke up in hospital not knowing what had happened. All I knew was I had scars and cuts all over me!

Amber Jackson (13)
Horndean Technology College

I'm Coming!

All that was heard was my breath and the faint footsteps gradually becoming louder and louder. But then they had suddenly vanished, what was going on? The curtains hiding me were pulled back; there he was. 'Ha, I've finally got you; it's your turn to count now!'

Charfi Pearson (14)
Horndean Technology College

A Strange Entrance

Suddenly, I found myself in a small room, there were no lights and no one was with me. It was completely silent; so silent that my heartbeat sounded unnaturally loud, as loud as a chainsaw. The horrific sound began to get louder and then my heart just stopped beating.

Lauren Sharp (15)
Horndean Technology College

Always Wear A Seat Belt

The needle split her skin. The liquid entered her veins. Her body shuddered as whispers crawled through her ears. Crying, screaming, her body wrapped tight, unable to breathe. Her eyes were blurred, everything unrecognisable. All she heard was a *beep, beep,* buzzing in her head. She awoke from the coma!

Harriet Sage (15)
Horndean Technology College

The Giant And The Child

A white-coated giant appeared from around
the corner. His eyes shone determinedly and he
advanced on the child, arms outstretched. The child
cowered in the corner as an iron hand gripped his
arm. He was pushed on to a chair, blinded by light.
'Open wide,' said the dentist.

Rhys Goddard (14)
Horndean Technology College

171

The Pursuit

As I continued to run, I looked behind me. There he was. I panicked, I began to sprint, my legs aching, fear gave me wings. I looked forward. So close to safety. He ran faster. He caught up with me. I slowed, filling with utter disbelief. Not second place again!

Wesley Abrahart (14)
Horndean Technology College

The Journey

Sat in the car, I was really bored and in one of those annoying moods. 'Are we there yet? I'm hungry. I need the toilet, I'm thirsty Mum, I'm bored.' The car ground to a grinding halt. Seat belts went off, we all got out. We had reached our final destination.

Kathryn Shinn (15)
Horndean Technology College

Gone

Me and my friend walking home from the park,
laughing and joking. She sees her boyfriend across
the road. There's always a busy road round here also
a zebra crossing. We wait, see no cars and cross. I'm
over, I look back, don't see her. She can't be … gone!

Emily Parr (15)
Horndean Technology College

The Bus

On the bus I sat. Four stops. Joined by a man, he wore blue. I dug into his mind, life. I learned a lot. Enough. He got off a stop before mine. What to do with the knowledge. Car maybe, plasma probably. I've always said work comes to you.

Tom Newman (14)
Horndean Technology College

The Plane

On the plane. Hours pass. The man next to me is fidgeting with fright on his face. A building is coming closer, closer. A blood-curdling scream comes from the captain's cabin. *Crash!*

Carla Mansbridge (14)
Horndean Technology College

At The Airport

At the airport hours passed. The plane to Cuba was five hours ago, I missed it! The next one was ten hours away. I was bored and tired. I fell asleep. Hours continued to pass. I woke up after a nightmare, I'd missed the plane again.

Kimberley Lynn (14)
Horndean Technology College

Was It A Ghost?

I entered the room, it was cold, dull, dark, empty.
No one else was to be seen. There was not a sound
just a whistling of wind in the distance. I looked
around, I saw a ghostly figure in the distance. As I
walked towards it to look, it disappeared.

Aimée Miller (14)
Horndean Technology College

178

Flanders Field

Hurried, worried, heart beating, running, shouting, shooting, thump. Stumbling, screaming, gurgling, bang. 'Attack, run, kill, bomb!'
Gunshot. I was floating, it seemed. Had the battle been won? Why? However. Why was I scared? I was entering the clouds. Saw something, began to wonder. Remembrance Day. I was dead.

Neale Madden (14)
Horndean Technology College

What Is It?

On my way walking to town. I stop to listen to screaming. There people go crashing past me running faster and faster. I look confused at them as they look at me. I stroll to the corner and peep around and there it is, but what it is? I run.

Elliot Siffs (14)

Horndean Technology College

Daydream

I'm flying above the world, parading the skies.
There's people, many people looking up at the sky
to watch me fly. Then I fall, I descend towards the
ground. I feel strange, mixes of exhilaration and
realisation of death. Inches from the ground.
'James, listen, maths is important!'

James Roberts (14)
Horndean Technology College

The Journey Of My Life

Bing-bong! 'Please can all passengers board the flight for Barcelona immediately.'
I got up, tired. I searched but they were nowhere to be found. Where had I put the tickets? Found them!
I got on the plane, sat down, drifted off ... 'Sir, wake up!'
Bing-bong! 'Welcome to Canada.'

Sophie Rippin (14)
Horndean Technology College

Humpty Dumpty

Humpty Dumpty sat on a wall. Humpty Dumpty had a great fall. None of the king's horses and none of the king's men even bothered. It was funny the first time, but now I think he just wants the attention.

Luke Ferre (14)
Horndean Technology College

To See Real Light

As it gets up it stretches, spreads out its wings to reveal the blends of colours. Opens its eyes for the first time and the light rushes to them, it shuts them again. Slowly opens them to see another, the same as itself. A red admiral, a butterfly.

Francesca Brockway (14)
Horndean Technology College

184

Mystery Guest

Alone in her mansion. Sitting quietly reading.
Suddenly a loud crash. She runs out to find it out.
Searching for the culprit. Footsteps getting louder.
Grabs the knife, stands ready. A figure appears
screaming … it's her husband.

Efin Thomas (14)
Horndean Technology College

185

What A Goal!

Goal! We scored the winning goal, it was great,
amazing. The adrenaline rushing through my mind, I
heard the roar of the frantic crowd. My teammates
leaping onto my shoulders. The fame I now have,
my own glory song. This is my team, where I belong.
What a goal!

Tom Scott (14)
Horndean Technology College

186

Little Devil

They stabbed into my flesh. Deeper and deeper and deeper. A drop of blood trickled down my arm. Then constant raking of my skin with sharp purposeful blades. I pleaded with my attacker, 'Please stop!' I will never poke my dog, Geoff, in the eye again.

Jack Sherlock (14)
Horndean Technology College

Rex The Pit Bull Terrier

Walking home from school. I kick number forty-two's gate. Anger. The pit bull terrier, but the gate's open. Rex sneers and starts chase. I spring up the hill, faster than I thought possible. Take cover in a coal bunker till the barking stops and I can go home. Embarrassed.

Charlotte Ludfam (14)
Horndean Technology College

188

Strange Cow

Strange. A cow in the street. Just wandering
aimlessly. Then it stops by the shop and squeezes
through the doorway. A minute later two men walk
out both of them downing a pint of milk. One holding
a fake cow's head, the other wearing a cow costume
on braces. Strange.

Elizabeth Peters (14)
Horndean Technology College

189

The Brother's Revenge

A dirty break-up, walking to the door with her ex-partner's possessions in her hand. The curious brother walked past 'Silver Necklace £50 On eBay'. He slipped it into his pocket. 'He won't need it, he left it in the box anyway.' It's the right thing to do.

Robert Green (14)
Horndean Technology College

Sausages

Everything's gone. Hope, light, imagination, all gone.
All of man's creations motionless. The bleached
bones of civilisation laid bare. Everything has ended.
What's that? Found! Everything's back! Under the
sofa, next to some smelly old sausages.

Gregory Marsden (14)
Horndean Technology College

The Inevitable Moment

The night before I was scared, but right then I was petrified. All my friends weren't, but I wasn't like them, I wasn't prepared. I knew it was inevitable, but I just wouldn't listen. I didn't spend my time wisely. Then, the dreaded moment arrived, 'Let the test begin … now.'

Jamie Knott (13)
Horndean Technology College

192

The Stairs

I felt nervous as I climbed down the long and winding stairs not knowing what was waiting for me at the bottom. As I got to the bottom there he was - the old man tied to the bars with chains.

Charlotte Moore (12)
Horndean Technology College

193

My Nightmare

After I just finished an amazing book I shut my eyes,
but heard something at the window. I shouted, 'Hey!'
He looked round and he held a knife at my heart
with aggression. My heart was going to explode.
Then I opened my eyes. Daylight? Was I dreaming?

Moffie King (13)
Horndean Technology College

Imagination

Black clouds overcame the clear starry night sky. Alone, there I was sitting on a log. I heard something rustling in the bushes behind me. It felt like something was holding my shoulder. It said something, but what was it? Maybe a ghost? Bird or is it just my imagination?

Nicki Blench (13)
Horndean Technology College

195

Pushing Away

I hated him but I never meant to kill him. He was always there. Taunting me, judging me. I pushed him away out of my life, out of my face. Then a shuddering crack of bone. I knew he was dead. My brother, dead!

Matthew Mould (12)
Horndean Technology College

The Pit

I was running, running like I've never run before.
Over the fence, through the ditch, up the hill and
then suddenly, the world was gone! A huge pit gaped
at me like a hungry mouth. I tumbled into this mouth.
Down, down, down. I crashed into the mud. What?
Ouch!

Jack Barton (13)
Horndean Technology College

Evacuated

The carriage pulls up to an antagonising halt. Hands clasped tightly. Everyone equipped with emergency supplies. Tear ducts filling and tight bonds broken. Alone. Turn your back on the past life and enter the carriage. Long corridor seems never-ending. Take an uncomfortable seat, wave goodbye. Will I ever return?

Samantha Pople (14)
Horndean Technology College

Fairy Tales

'No such thing as fairy tales,' she sneered.
Molly sat in her glittering net dress, gauze wings, limp
with no frame; fluttering. She looked at the world
through rose-coloured glasses. Leah was practical,
she ripped the tiara from Molly's head.
'Plastic.' Molly reddened.
'Not like mine, mine's real magic!'

Joanne McManus (14)
Horndean Technology College

199

Misplaced Optimism

Frank, an amateur handyman, was a confirmed optimist. An excessive smoker, he didn't believe he was susceptible to heart attacks or lung cancer. One day there was a gas leak in his kitchen and Frank, cigarette in hand, went to fix it. He was right. He didn't die of either.

Victoria Hockin (14)
Horndean Technology College

200

The Day That Monday Dawned

All week I waited but this day it came. Getting out of bed, I trudged down the stairs. 'Mum, I feel sick,' I moaned.

'Oh come on dear,' she replied.

The hour drew nearer and nearer … the roar of the engine, screeching of tyres. It was Monday at school.

Luke Carter-Lockwood (12)

Horndean Technology College

The Broken Spaceship

Blinded by the light in my spaceship. The big colourful sun was getting dangerously close. 'Turn the other way!' They tugged hard on the steering device. Then unluckily it broke off. Chaos was caused as they flew into the burning red sun.

Moffy O Neiff (12)
Horndean Technology College

The Journey

The day was long and tiring but finally we're here. We journeyed across the border of Scotland to England and over the English countryside. We crawled across the Channel with its raging, angry waves and eventually we got to France. I wish they had a faster plane for our journey.

Lucy Affery (12)
Horndean Technology College

Hangman's Noose

If I was born just 500 years ago, I surely would be swinging from the hangman's noose. But now I'm free, free as can be. Free as a flea. My velvet robe floats around me as I stand alone, staring down the barrel of the hangman's noose. Cold, soft hands.

Richard Bowpitt (14)
Horndean Technology College

John's Day Out!

John was walking along the road when an apple fell on his head.
'Is the sky falling down? I must go tell the king!'
John was a simple child, easily pleased and was not the sharpest knife in the drawer. On his way to the king a bus hit him.

Laura Caine (14)
Horndean Technology College

Untitled

'We there yet Mum?'
'No, I've told you we've got another hour yet!'
It was like that all the time on their yearly roadtrip,
arguing and getting frustrated. Not that anyone
wanted to go anyway. It quickly became dark,
animals were out, their brakes squeaked. Their trip
was over.

Paige Sawyer (14)
Horndean Technology College

Happy Holiday

Something was wrong. Driving through the country lanes was extremely spooky and everything was telling me not to go. Still, we all arrived at the campsite with all our items. After we set up the tent, we went for an evening stroll in the woods. We never got out alive.

Alex Ware (13)
Horndean Technology College

207

Moon Dreams

He landed on the moon.
No one thought I could do it, he thought.
He jumped, surprised by the amount of gravity. Up,
then suddenly down into the monster's mouth. In he
went feeling no pain.
'Argh!' and suddenly he wakes up.
His wife says, 'Just another moon dream!'

Jessica Hann (12)
Horndean Technology College

208

The Light

It was dark. I was alone and lost. My journey for long-forgotten peace had only just begun. The funeral had finished, no one was here for me any longer. But I struggled on. Taking lefts and rights before I saw it … the light shining bright. I was finally home!

Kyle Shinn (12)
Horndean Technology College

Facing My Fear

Nervousness had overwhelmed me, there were butterflies in my stomach, my hands were sweaty. I was thinking what to do, should I run? If I run my mum would flip, she'd say, 'When am I going to get it?' No, I'll face it! I gave her my school report.

George Summers (12)
Horndean Technology College

Our Humble Host

Living on adrenaline, others; too weak. Unable to evade the sweeping wave of termination. Their last moments of trepidation sprawled across their faces like scrambled egg on toast. Segregation: inevitable, death greatly anticipated. Apparently we're 'contagious' but they'll never catch us. Sonic clamour of the nozzle. Too late … flea spray!

Hannah Jones (14)
Horndean Technology College

211

An Era Behind?

Happy Mondays? Seriously? It's not a happy Monday today. My first day at my new school. I get up early and slip on my best outfit. Will I fit in? I leave with my favourite feather boa around my neck, pink platforms on and my hair styled in a pineapple!

Sarah Oliver (13)
Horndean Technology College

212

Magical Space

As I raced into space, every breath was pulled out of me. I was speechless as I looked around and saw this new glittering view on the world. I felt so amazed and special as I glanced into the distance. It made me wonder what is out there? I wonder …

Olivia White (13)
Horndean Technology College

213

Ocean View

The ice-cold water pierced my skin as I jumped into a new world. The colourful arrangement of reefs and citizens was blinding. The city amazed me. The fish bustled and hurried around as if late for work. *Bang!* A large black figure appeared on the horizon. It's the end.

Vanessa Kinsley (12)
Horndean Technology College

214

Forbidden Love

Two families. Forsaken to an eternity of hate and violence. But what if you take one from each family and end up with a baby? What happens to the little guy? Make it easy for him? Nah! Let's bring him up in a world of destruction and watch the outcome.

Lucy Green (13)
Horndean Technology College

215

It's Time

It's time. Five years training in immense pressure.
We must get back what we lost. We are hungry for
revenge and will stop at nothing to win. We will eat
our way to glory and shall not be killed at any cost.
We will eat the most pies to win.

Robert Rowney (13)
Horndean Technology College

216

Worst Day Ever!

I opened my front door, fumbling with the key as the alcohol rushed to my head. Finally, it decided to open and I staggered through the door. I'd had such a bad day, worked long hours, kicked out of the pub. I walked into the bedroom and *she* was gone.

Tom Morgan (12)
Horndean Technology College

Massacre

The dark sky hung over the battlefield. The millions of Englishmen looked straight into the eyes of the German fighters. A little later cries could be heard miles away of people clashing and screaming out with pain. The sun shone proudly over the victorious Englishmen as they strolled away.

Matthew Wakeham (13)
Horndean Technology College

The Proud Englishmen

The grey sky loomed over the battlefield. The thousands of Englishmen gazed bravely into the eyes of the French. Minutes later there was screaming and roaring of people dying. The stars shone proudly over the victorious English army as they marched away after a very, very gruesome and tiring night.

Oliver Barlow (13)
Horndean Technology College

Surprise!

I walked into a dark room, nothing else was there except me. I could hear the wind whistling outside. Rain hammered on the roof. I then heard footsteps getting closer. *Bang! Bang!* Rattling of chains. They were coming for me. The door opened. *Slam!* I couldn't see, who was it?

Chris Waterson (12)
Horndean Technology College

All Pretty Roses Have Sharp Thorns

The dog lifted her head, her glossy red hair falling over her white face. She looked to the outside world as a soft breeze rustled in through the dogflap. A passing bystander stroked her, pushing her hair off her face, then shrieking at her.
It was hard being eyeless …

Katie Robinson (12)
Horndean Technology College

The Shop

I was panting like a dog. My legs couldn't carry my
already given up body. I was quivering. Surely they
couldn't make me do any more. Then, 'Come on
Dad, it's only down to the shop.'
This didn't help my already jittery nerves.
Then, 'OK Dad, I got the milk.'

Kieron Young (13)
Horndean Technology College

Reaching The Limit

My heart skipped a frantic beat. The enormity of what I had done had not yet sunk in. I looked over the breathtaking horizon. My dream had become a reality, my goal had been fulfilled. I punched the air in delight. I had finally cooked the perfect egg!

Dominic Nozahic (13)
Horndean Technology College

The Word

There it is, that word again. The one word that can frustrate and anger any who walk. My eardrums burst. My brain boils. My legs shake in fury and distress. The one and only word. It drives me to the edge of madness, the screaming, shouting. The word, *'no'!*

Michael Smith (13)
Horndean Technology College

House Of Living Death

Alone. Rain hammering. Moon black. I'm terrified, solitary, curled in hiding. House's bones creaking, impression of an eerie presence. Flickering lightning elongating shadows, suddenly black, nothing! *Thud! Thud!* A heart, mine or the house?
I sprint, screaming, slipping. Chilling metal pierces, heart stops, pounding continues! Immortal, blood-curdling. *'Argh!'*

David Giffott (14)
Horndean Technology College

Kitchen Killer

Drip, drip, drip. He walked into the kitchen. *Thump!* The kettle fell over. *Thump!* The toaster. *Thump!* The air froze around him. His limbs stuck together. *Slam!* The door locked behind him. The drawer flung open. An invisible hand lifted the knife. The cold steel stilled his beating heart.

Cesene Curry (15)
Horndean Technology College

226

Untitled

I am a little tiny bacteria trying to stop people coming to school so they cannot do their GCSEs and so they can fail them. I have formed my own army of bacteria. I am soon to take over the world. I crawl into their food and then double.

John Ratcliffe (14)
Horndean Technology College

227

One Day

One day in a dark and scary wood was a noise. It sounded like a grumbling sound. One day we made a trap and placed it in the wood with some meat in. Then we waited. Then we heard that sound. We ran to the cave - it was a wolf.

Ben Haines (13)
Horndean Technology College

228

A Plagued Life

Half the people down my street have it, their houses boarded up, left to rot, shrivel up. No one talks to anyone else anymore. Ashamed, lonely, hopeless, drowned in death. Quiet filling the room as the nails dig into the wood. Another life wasted away, but this time it's mine.

Megan Comfay (13)
Horndean Technology College

Football Wall

On a Tuesday afternoon Humpty Dumpty was playing football on the council estate kicking it against the garages. When he accidentally kicked it over the wall and smashed a greenhouse. So he ran to his house but no one was in so he climbed the wall and slipped. *Crash, crack!*

Conor Hillier (14)
Horndean Technology College

Resistance Is Futile

Surrounded. No escape. Frostbite claimed my fingers. So cold, blood trickling from my hand froze before dripping to the floor. Allied Forces attacked. Myself, my comrades, watched as our fellow friends fell under their unstoppable onslaught. Sergeant Stubb was hit, blood poured racing to the floor. He's dead. Resistance, futile!

James Devine (14)
Horndean Technology College

In The Woods

Little girl in the woods, looking for her friend. Friend lost, scared, needing help. Gloomy voices saying, 'I'm going to get you!'
Trees swaying in the wind. Her friend was never found. Girl screamed in fear. Voices still echoing all around. It was like the trees were talking to her.

Rebecca Dennis (14)
Horndean Technology College

Bullied

Alone. Sad, unhappy eyes peer down at me. Scared, worried, a punch, a kick. Falling to the ground. Bullied. Made to feel upset, angry and low. A waster, a fool and a no one. No one to talk to. There's one thing to say and that's - bullied.

Matthew Creamer (13)
Horndean Technology College

233

We Saw It

'What's that in the water?'
'Dunno, let's go look.'
We went to see what was lurking in the water. A
massive eel-shaped monster swam past the shore,
poked its head out the water. We ran into town. 'We
saw the Loch Ness monster.'
Nobody believed us. We saw it!

Samuel Lyndon (14)
Horndean Technology College

The Bus

Sat on the bus reading my book. Suspicious character
asked, 'Anyone sitting here?'
'No.'
He kept looking at my bag. I thought nothing of it.
He was shuffling his feet, fidgeting. He was weird but
I wasn't really bothered. The next stop he got off. My
bag was gone.

Lauren Doughty (14)
Horndean Technology College

The Forbidden Room

It was a dark and cold room with no one in it. One door and one window with a 'Danger' sign above the door. One person wanted to go in, something told him to go in, but he didn't know if he wanted to. He entered but never came out!

Bethany Middlecoate (13)
Horndean Technology College

236

The Great Gum Incident

Silence - then a blood-curdling scream protruding from the darkness. As I edge towards the doorway, I can hear a girl weeping as she is shaken roughly. A silhouette emerges from the shadows, brandishing weapons of mass destruction. 'Honestly, your sister's only gone and got gum stuck in her hair!' … Eww!

Bethany Sutton (12)
Oaklands Catholic School

Missing!

Punch! I was bleeding. I then realised I was missing something important, very important. I looked on the floor, I looked in my pocket, in my hands ... I looked on the sofa ... it was nowhere to be found. I looked on the floor again and saw it - my tooth!

Oliver Dasmut-Rudd (12)
Oaklands Catholic School

238

Sleeper

Starting hardest task of life. Pushing high, warm blankets surrounding, blinding lights flash, pillows tugged, terror strikes, endless ringing screams like Sleeping Beauty. I wake. Shouting sounds, 'Get up now!' Soft surroundings, warm. Cuddly toys, arms swing madly across room. Blinking eyes spring open wide, getting out of my bed.

Clare Trevenna (12)

Oaklands Catholic School

239

Famous Last Words . . .

Whoever finds my saga: I am a soldier. Black rats gnaw my feet. Blood in my mouth, dripping; cold steel of my rifle rests against my blue cheek. My brave friends are dead. Soon it will be my turn. Fields of gas. Whistles blow. Now I can join my friends …

Cormac Fosey (11)
Oaklands Catholic School

240

Experiencing Black

The darkness seemed alive. It gave no hints or clues.
I saw miles of nothing. It haunted, it teased, it never
seemed to leave. Then a sound. Phew, just the cat!
Wait - I don't have a cat. It came back again - the
feeling. Mum, please fix the night-light!

Gabrielle Roxby (12)
Oaklands Catholic School

The Nightmare Garden

Cunningly they attack, unnoticed, for weeks. They bear down on my precious, knocking down everything in their path. Their numbers increase steadily. I gather my weapons, ready to attack single-handedly. They fight back. Temporarily, I surrender to get my next weapon. My garden is now protected by ... weed killer!

Emily Schonhut (12)
Oaklands Catholic School

242

Don't Chase Me

I was still running. I could feel the hot breath prickling at my neck - he was catching up, so I sprinted faster. Suddenly, the black wall appeared right in front of me. I quickly swerved, looked back - he, too, had got past the wall. I tripped. Then he shouted, 'Tag!'

Sophie Peach (12)
Oaklands Catholic School

243

Bad Idea

I had an idea. 'Hi!' I said to the guy.
'Hello.'
'Nice laptop,' I exclaimed.
'Thank you, it's very hi-tech.'
We chatted on.
'Look, it's the two-headed Flintstones,' I shouted.
I snatched the laptop and ran.
'Sucker,' I called out when I looked back.
Bang! Uh-oh, I hit a wall.

Jetcy James (12)
Oaklands Catholic School

Untitled

We were waiting 15-30 minutes then the dentist's secretary called me in for my check-up. It was time to face the truth. The secretary told me to take a seat whilst the dentist came in with blood all over his apron from the last patient … or was it?

Kieyran Kelly (12)
Oaklands Catholic School

245

Squeak!

Oh no, Mum fell asleep last night on the sofa. Rats were out, now they're inside the sofa and we can't get them out! Tried tempting them out - won't work. There's only a tiny gap. We'll have to make it bigger and bigger. Wait, what's that on my back? *Squeak!*

Jennifer Goldsmith (12)
Oaklands Catholic School

246

Holimprekdoo Park

In the land of far, far away, Dec and Fiona were queuing at the Kwik-E-Mart when Warren ran in and stole a yoghurt. Scooby-Doo, the guard dog, ran out and barked madly at Warren. When the shopkeeper who turned out to be Cartman shouted, 'Oh my god, he killed Kenny!'

Tiffy Newman (12)
Wildern School

247

Ponytails

Murphy galloped around calling for his mate. Murphy suddenly flattened out and charged towards the gate … he was flying, the wind whipped through his mane and tail. He was free! Murphy charged down the track towards the yard, his feet pounding. Then he found what he wanted - his best mate!

Georgina Jenks (12)
Wildern School

Getting Ready

Coming in from school. Looking forward to the night ahead. So many things had to be done, hair make-up and food. The party was going to be great. 'Oh no, my hair's gone curly!' was the cry. Under drawers trying to find hair straighteners. Hope it doesn't go wrong!

Becki Young (12)
Wildern School

Untitled

I sat with my hand in his, his other brushing against my cheek. I felt the warm beat of his heart as he pulled me closer. He whispered sweet words in my ear. I knew this was the moment he was supposed to kiss me; he slapped me, 'You're dumped!'

Steph Barfoot (12)
Wildern School

The Magic Forest

I walked into a misty forest to walk my dog. I heard a whistling noise in the background. Then suddenly I felt something lean over me, a cool breeze of wind passed by. I looked around, there was nothing there. Then my dog howled and echoed around me.

Georgina Lenfon (12)
Wildern School

Poodle Sandwich

'Mum, Mum, can I have a poodle? I'll look after it and feed it.'
'OK, we'll go to Sue, she breeds them.'
'I'll call it Fluffy.' They took it home. When she was at school it got out, went to the road. Dog plus car equals not good.

Sophie Buckland (12)
Wildern School

252

The Phone Call

I was walking down the road and my phone went off.
'Hello.'
'Meet me at your house in ten minutes.'
Ten minutes later I was at home. A knock was at the
door. There was a mysterious man there. He walked
into the house. He then pulled out a knife.

Luke Diaper (12)
Wildern School

253

There's A Monster Under My Bed

At 12 I suddenly woke up to hear a big, greasy, loud growl under my bed. So I got out of my bed and looked under. I suddenly heard the noise again. I saw it, it was a scary monster. So I knew it was the end of my life.

Thomas Dafey (11)
Wildern School

254

Stranded?

The TARDIS was thrown to the edge of the universe falling through the vortex. It spun. It finally crashed and the Doctor and Martha felt the TARDIS skid and hit a rock.

'The vortex's dead,' yelled the Doctor.

'We're stranded,' screamed Martha. She looked outside the TARDIS. It was …

Daniel Court (12)

Wildern School

255

Boom

Two men: guns in their hands. Bomb in the middle.
Gun loaded, they aimed. One moved back, one
moved forward. It was tense. Cops around every
corner. Seconds until the bomb would go off. One
moved the gun down to the floor. One still had it
aimed. Seconds left. *Boom!*

Sam Pritchard (11)
Wildern School

The Grated Cheese

It sits in the fridge corner waiting to be collected by the human being. Its wrapping tight around the cheese. Finally the fridge door opens, the cheese was moved from its ice-cold corner. The cheese opens his eyes and he found himself on a grating board - dead, laying down.

Callum Paddock (12)
Wildern School

Untitled

The child reached for a book on the highest shelf. He looked at the front cover and pulled up a seat. He started to read the opening page. A couple of pages later he became hypnotised by the words. Suddenly, a flash appeared and he was in a big jungle.

James Watson-McKendrick (14)
Wildern School

The Wood

I was running so fast trying to get out. He was catching up. I turned in a different direction. I was out of breath. I sat down behind a tree. I heard him coming. I felt a tap on my shoulder then I turned around but no one was there.

Gemma Smith (14)
Wildern School

The Chase

Hearing footsteps pound behind me, clenching my
fists, the wind rushing through my ears, my heart
pounding and my breakfast hurtling up towards my
throat. Running faster, falling and grazing both knees,
I could hardly see; my eyes filled with water and
tears streaming down my cheeks. Running a race.

Georgia Soffe (14)
Wildern School

260

Giving The Wrong Impression

I was getting nervous and didn't know what to do. I started stroking her thigh, heard her moan as I grasped her breast but all was fine. All at once the white stuff came. It's all done, it's all over now. My very first time at milking a cow, yes!

Martin Affen (14)
Wildern School

261

The Zoo

I pull up to the gates, it's a horrible smell. There's different noises, the shapes are different sizes. You cannot think, they're put in cages. Some dangerous, some harmful. You can buy some food and feed them. You see some sleeping, you can see some eating. I'm at the zoo.

Ryan Smith (14)
Wildern School

The Ruck

There was a massive bundle - punches were thrown.
Men were staring at each other. Blood on their shirts.
The bundle collapsed. Men were laying on each
other in pain. They got up, ran into a huddle again.
One of them bit the man's ear in this rough rugby
match.

Tom Dicker (14)

Wildern School

Happy Hallowe'en

Vampires, monsters, murderers and werewolves all after one thing. They have to get as much as they can before the night turns to day and before everyone goes to sleep. I must not tell anyone where I got all these eyeballs on sticks.

Ding-dong, 'Thank you, happy Hallowe'en. Goodnight.'

Ryan Vickery (13)
Wildern School

Zooming

It's coming, I hear it. The roars and screams in the distance. It's ready to pounce. I know it's going to creep up on me. Lightning fast and looks like the beast. Although, I'm not scared. Then I see it, the car is fast and sounds great! I love it!

Curtis Pitter (14)
Wildern School

Toilet Throne

As I am sat on my throne I felt a rush of weight relieved from my body, escaping at 100mph, flung out of me like a torpedo, sliding along the bowl. As I reach for the silver handle and flush, she floats round and round the toilet bowl.

Laurence Taplin (13)
Wildern School

Payback

She said she was really sorry, it was too late. She begged me to forgive her, it was time to get the bully back. It was her turn to know how it feels. I screamed at her, the bus came. A squeal of brakes, but why did I save her?

Amber Richards (12)
Wildern School

Friday Night

It was Friday night and everyone was getting ready to go out! Everyone except Tarra! She had an argument with her brother earlier that day and her parents were fuming and had grounded her. She stormed up the stairs, sat on her bed. It wasn't fair, he always wins!

Lucia Hunton (12)
Wildern School

The Chase

I ran - nothing else mattered any more, would it get me? After all I've been through. No! I can't think about that now. Its disgusting brown fingernail reached out for me, it was getting closer. It's going to get me. No! This is it, I'm caught. 'Tag, you're it!' 'Damn!'

Tom Underwood (12)

Wildern School

It's Now Mine!

Bright ... colourful ... vibrant ... stared right at me.
It caught my eye that two sets were locked on the
same thing. Sweat sailed down; heart beats grew.
'I will win, I will purchase!' It's my turn to grow a
smirk, not hers. A turned mat tripped her up. It's
now *mine!*

Emma-Louise Stansaff (12)
Wildern School

The Butterfly

I was alone at home. The house was silent except from the pitter-patter of the rain. I then spotted the most beautiful colourful thing perching on the window sill! I opened the window. In came the most wonderful butterfly. It landed on my hand but then flew away again.

Charlotte Payne (12)
Wildern School

The Poor Microphone

You could tell as soon as she stepped up on the stage that this was her calling, as if singing had some deep meaning to her. Everything was perfect, she was beautiful. You could see the passion in her eyes. All was set, she opened her mouth and began singing. Ouch!

Kelfy Blackburn (11)
Wildern School

The Anger Within

His eyes were cold, menacing and filled with rage.
The anger that had been created by me. From
anybody else's eyes it would have at least been
over by now. I'd pushed him before, but not to this
extent. I opened my eyes ready for what was coming
next.

Chantelle Skifton (12)
Wildern School

273

Out Of Bounds

Hallowe'en night. She crept down the stairs into her grandpa's dark and dingy basement. As she edged forwards, she could hear a faint whispering. She turned slowly to see two piercing green eyes glaring at her. She ran, she ran faster than ever before. Too bad it wasn't fast enough …

Alexandra Beard (12)
Wildern School

The Devil!

I tiptoed up the stairs prepared for anything that would jump out unexpectedly. I slowly turned the handle of the door. At the top of the stairs I slowly took a look around advancing through boxes and cupboards. I turned around. There, right in front of me was the Devil.

Cara Afdous Boyes (12)
Wildern School

The Cute Monster!

As I walked through the woods I heard rustling behind me, I was scared. Then I started to run, I was panting now, hard. Something stood on a dead branch which made me jump. Then suddenly a white fluffy cat jumped out in front of me. I took him home!

Jade Jones (12)
Wildern School

276

Home Alone!

I heard the door slam. I was home alone with no one to talk to. I didn't know what to do so I quickly hid behind the curtain in the living room. I heard heavy footsteps getting closer and closer. I peeked through the curtain and there was a gorilla!

Sarah Barker (12)
Wildern School

277

The Deadly Bush

The pumpkin lanterns flickered, making the cold night sky look like an all red, yellow and orange firework display. On the ground … sweets. A long trail of colourful sweets led to the thorn bush at the side of the path. The bush rustled and wept, covered in dark red blood.

Caroline Sait (12)
Wildern School

My New Arm

'Laura?'
Laura opened her eyes and looked around. She was in hospital. Before she was in the streets as a car hit her … 'What happened?' Laura whispered.
A doctor spoke, 'We've had to give you a bionic arm.'
Laura stared at her metal implant wondering how different this would be.

Kim Barrett-Warren (12)
Wildern School

Untitled

I was alone. The rain tapped on the window of my bedroom. Suddenly, the angry rain smacked the window like a punch. I placed my hand on the glass. A misty outline of steam covered my fingerprints like a shadow. I was afraid it would come back to me again.

Effie Simpson (12)
Wildern School

The Creak

I'm in the lounge watching TV. I'm getting tired. I get up to go to bed and then I hear a creak, even though there's no one on the old creaky stairs. I wonder what it could be, the cat, the dog? I go to the stairs, the creak stops!

Stuart Cornwall (11)
Wildern School

281

The Race

It was the big day, Mickey and his friends were limbering up at the starting line. Side to side, up and down. The official had said on your marks, *Bang!* The race had started and we were running. Mickey then Donald, Donald then Mickey and Goofy still at the line …

Nick Blair (12)
Wildern School

Information

We hope you have enjoyed reading this book - and that you
will continue to enjoy it in the coming years.
If you like reading and writing, drop us a line or give us a call
and we'll send you a free information pack. Alternatively visit
our website at www.youngwriters.co.uk

Write to:
Young Writers Information,
Remus House,
Coltsfoot Drive,
Peterborough,
PE2 9JX
Tel: (01733) 890066
Email: youngwriters@forwardpress.co.uk